A First Flight® Level Three Reader

Matthew
and the
Midnight
Firefighter

By Allen Morgan

Illustrated by
Michael Martchenko

Fitzhenry & Whiteside

Published as a FirstFlight®Reader by Fitzhenry & Whiteside 2003

Fitzhenry & Whiteside, 195 Allstate Parkway, Markham, Ontario L3R 4T8

In the United States, 121 Harvard Avenue, Suite 2, Allston, Massachusetts 02134

www.fitzhenry.ca   godwit@fitzhenry.ca.

10 9 8 7 6 5 4 3 2 1

First published in 2000 by Stoddart Kids
Matthew and the Midnight Firefighter

National Library of Canada Cataloguing in Publication Data

Morgan, Allen, 1946-
[Matthew and the midnight firefighter]
A wild midnight adventure / by Allen Morgan ;
illustrated by Michael Martchenko.

(A first flight level three reader)
Previously published under the title: Matthew and the midnight firefighter.
ISBN 1-55041-875-0 (bound)—ISBN 1-55041-877-7 (pbk.)

I. Martchenko, Michael II. Title.
III. Title: Matthew and the midnight firefighter.
IV. Series: First flight reader.

PS8576.O642M264 2003   jC813'.54   C2003-902337-0
PZ7

U.S. Publisher Cataloging-in-Publication Data
(Library of Congress Standards)

Morgan, Allen, 1946-
A wild midnight adventure / by Allen Morgan ;
illustrated by Michael Martchenko.—1st ed.
[40] p. : col. ill. ; cm. (A first flight: level three reader)
Originally published as: Matthew and the midnight firefighter ;
Toronto: Stoddart, 2000.
Summary: After celebrating the Fourth of July, Matthew heads for bed
but ends up joining Fast Eddie and the midnight firefighters, as well as
a group of turkeys, in patrolling the city for fires.
ISBN 1-55041-875-0
ISBN 1-55041-877-7 (pbk.)
1. Firefighters — Fiction. 2. Fourth of July — Fiction.
I. Martchenko, Michael, ill. II. Series. III. Title.
[E] 21   PZ7.M8203Wil 2003

Fitzhenry & Whiteside acknowledges with thanks the Canada Council for the Arts,
the Government of Canada through the Book Publishing Industry Development
Program (BPIDP), the Ontario Arts Council and the Government of Ontario
through the Ontario Media Development Corporation's Ontario Book Initiative
for their support for our publishing program.

Printed in Hong Kong

Design by Wycliffe Smith Design Inc.

CHAPTER ONE

When July began, the weather turned
hot just in time for the holidays.
Matthew decided he might cool down if
he was a firefighter.

Matthew put on his mother's garden-
ing boots and grabbed the vacuum hose.
He was just getting good at his siren
noises when he heard his mother's call.

"The barbecue's ready! Come down
and eat!"

For dinner they had hot dogs with lots of catsup on top. There were chips and dips, and lemonade. Matthew's mother put out a bowl of raw veggies too. She explained they were chock full of vitamins, so Matthew had quite a few.

After dinner Matthew toasted marshmallows over the coals. He tried to be careful and brown them evenly all around. But it didn't work out the way he planned. Every single marshmallow caught on fire.

"Those coals stay hot for a very long time," Matthew said.

Chapter Two

When it was time for bed, Matthew began to worry. "Did you put out the coals in the barbecue, Mom? You have to use lots of water to make sure they are really out."

"Yes, I did," said his mother. "I was very careful." She turned out the light and kissed him goodnight.

Matthew lay awake for a while. He heard the sounds of holiday fireworks exploding in the night.

"A rocket has to be aimed just right," he told himself as he fell asleep. "If it lands someplace by mistake, it could start a fire just like the coals in our barbecue."

Matthew woke up at the stroke of midnight. Outside, the sky was filled with fireworks. He watched for a while, but then he felt thirsty. He went to the bathroom to get a drink.

When Matthew returned to his room, he saw a big red rocket fly in through the window. He quickly used his glass of water to put out the flames.

Chapter Three

A few moments later a firefighter climbed in through the window.

"Good thinking, kid! You did the right thing and you did it fast. You could be a great firefighter. Why don't you join my team? Fast Eddie's the name, fighting fire's the game."

Matthew agreed and they shook on the deal. Then Fast Eddie's pager began to blink red.

Beep-beep! Beep-beep! Beeeeeeep!

"Come on!" Fast Eddie cried. "That's a call from the fire hall. Grab your boots. Let's go!"

Fast Eddie ran to the stairs and jumped on the railing. Matthew did too. As they slid down, Fast Eddie clicked a switch on his beeper. A secret door opened at the foot of the stairs. *Swoooooosh!* They went sliding on through.

They slid past the basement and into the ground, then up and down and around and around until they came out at the fire hall. All the other firefighters were ready to go. Fast Eddie and Matthew jumped on the truck.

CHAPTER FOUR

They drove the truck to the fireworks store. The midnight turkeys were all outside. "We knew you would come if we called!" They cried. "Come dance with us. It's easy to do. We'll show you how!"

They stuck out their tongues and wiggled their bums. Then they danced around until they fell down.

Fast Eddie frowned. "It looks like a holiday barbecue," he told Matthew. "I just hope they are careful."

"We are always careful about what we eat," the turkeys said. "To bring out the best in a marshmallow you put lots of catsup on top. Then all you need is a good roasting stick."

One of the turkeys stuck a marshmallow on the end of a rocket and held it over the coals.

"No!" shouted Matthew. "Don't do that!"

But it was too late.

The rocket took off with a mighty *Hisssssss* and flew through the window of the store.

A great explosion rocked the air as all the fireworks inside the store were lit. Seconds later the fireworks were everywhere.

KABLOOM!

KABLOONG!

Fat, gluey gobs of sticky marshmallow goo fell like rain from the sky.

"Wow!" the turkeys cried. "This is the best show we've ever had!"

CHAPTER FIVE

One of the rockets fell onto the roof, and a fire broke out. There was no time to lose.

Matthew grabbed the fire hose and jumped onto Fast Eddie's back. Fast Eddie carried him up the ladder. The hose whirled around like an angry snake, but Matthew held on. He sprayed water all over the roof. In no time at all the fire was out.

The turkeys cheered as Matthew and the midnight firefighter came down the ladder.

"Kid, you're the best," Fast Eddie said, and he taped a big star on Matthew's chest. "I'm making you the new Assistant Midnight Fire Chief!"

The turkeys were sticky with marshmallow goo, so they borrowed the hose.

"Pass the shampoo. We need lots of bubbles," they told Matthew. "We're sorry about the trouble with the rockets and all. It will never, ever, happen again...at least for a while."

"Sorry is not enough, I'm afraid," Fast Eddie said. "A fire is a serious matter. You will have to work to pay for the damage."

"Work?" gasped the turkeys.

"You could make them firefighters," Matthew suggested.

Fast Eddie grinned. "That's a perfect plan. Since they were the ones that started this fire, they can help us put out a few others."

The turkeys cheered. They jumped up onto the fire truck, rang the bell, and turned on the siren.

"We're here for you!" they cried.

Chapter Six

Matthew and the midnight firefighters drove all through the streets. They sprayed water everywhere. Soon the whole city was soaking wet.

They gobbled marshmallows as they worked.

"Eat them all; they are good for you," Fast Eddie said with a grin. "Marshmallows give you energy, and they have a few vitamins, too."

The last stop was Matthew's back-yard. Everyone soaked the coals in the barbecue. Matthew was a bit sleepy, so he said goodnight.

"You're a natural, kid," Fast Eddie said. "Come out and fight fires whenever you like."

Matthew climbed up the ladder to his bedroom. Soon he was fast asleep.

Matthew woke up at the crack of dawn. He put on his boots and went down the hall to give his mother a glass of water. Her eyes were still closed, so he held the glass above her head. A few drips fell down onto her chin.

Matthew's mother opened one eye. "I don't think I'm that thirsty right now," she said.

CHAPTER SEVEN

Later, Matthew and his mother went downstairs.

"It rained a lot last night," said his mother.

"That wasn't rain; that was me," Matthew said. "Fast Eddie helped me with the hose. We had a big truck and we drove it all around. The whole city got soaking wet."

His mother was still sleepy, so Matthew set the table. Then he opened a bag of marshmallows.

"Breakfast is ready," Matthew announced. "Fast Eddie says that marshmallows are an important food."

"Marshmallows?" his mother said. "For breakfast?"

"Don't worry, Mom. We don't have to use the barbecue. We don't even have to cook them at all.

"Like you always say, things have way more vitamins if you eat them raw."

FIRST FLIGHT®

FIRST FLIGHT® is an exciting
new series of beginning readers.
The series presents titles which include songs,
poems, adventures, mysteries, and humor
by established authors and illustrators.
FIRST FLIGHT® makes the introduction to
reading fun and satisfying
for the young reader.

FIRST FLIGHT® is available in 4 levels
to correspond to reading development.

Level 1 – Pre-school - Grade 1
Large type, repetition of simple concepts that are perfect
for reading aloud, easy vocabulary and endearing
characters in short simple stories for the earliest reader.

Level 2 – Grade 1 - Grade 3
Longer sentences, higher level of vocabulary, repetition,
and high-interest stories for the progressing reader.

Level 3 – Grade 2 - Grade 4
Simple stories with more involved plots and a simple
chapter format for the newly independent reader.

Level 4 – Grade 3 - up (First Flight Chapter Books)
More challenging level, minimal illustrations for the
independent reader.